• NOTE TO CHILD •

Get ready to count! Are you excited? You should be. All the numbers from 1 to 25 are on the cards beneath this one and you are going to learn them all. Use the pictures to help you learn and be sure to ask questions if you have any.

Are you all set? Well then, let's

FLIP OVER

to the number 1 and have some fun!

one wagon

- Say the number out loud.
- How many wagons do you see?
- Use your finger to write the number in the air.
- What is 1 plus 1?
- What would you like to fill this wagon with?
- What number comes next?

one wagon

I

two ducklings

2

- Say the number out loud.
- Count the ducklings.
- Use your finger to write the number in the air.
- What is 2 plus 2?
- How would a duck count to 2?
- What number comes next?

two ducklings

2

three rabbits

3

- Say the number out loud.

- Count the rabbits.

- Use your finger to write the number in the air.

- Find three of something in this room.

- Can you show me three fingers?

- What number comes next?

three rabbits

3

four forks

- Say the number out loud.
- Count the forks.
- Use your finger to write the number in the air.
- How many points are there on each fork?
- What would you like to eat with a fork right now?
- What number comes next?

four forks

4

five toy trucks

5

- Say the number out loud.
- Count the toy trucks.
- Use your finger to write the number in the air.
- How many different colors are on each truck?
- How many of the trucks do not have black wheels?
- What number comes next?

five toy trucks

5

six stop signs

STOP STOP STOP
STOP STOP STOP

- Say the number out loud.
- Count the stop signs.
- Use your finger to write the number in the air.
- How many sides are on each stop sign?
- Can you hold your breath for 6 seconds?
- What number comes next?

six stop signs

seven puppies

7

- Say the number out loud.
- Count the puppies.
- Use your finger to write the number in the air.
- Let's name the puppies.
- How many of the puppies are lying down?
- What number comes next?

seven puppies

eight walnuts

8

- Say the number out loud.
- Count the walnuts.
- Use your finger to write the number in the air.
- Here's a joke:
  Why was the number 6 so sad?
  Because 7 ate 9. (7,8,9)
- Can you show me 8 fingers?
- What number comes next?

eight walnuts

nine chompers

9

- Say the number out loud.
- Count the chompers.
- Use your finger to write the number in the air.
- Count the teeth in your mouth.
- How many times a day do you brush your teeth?
- What number comes next?

nine chompers

ten butterflies

10

- Say the number out loud.
- Count the butterflies.
- Use your finger to write the number in the air.
- Count from 1 to 10 out loud.
- How many yellow butterflies do you see?
- What number comes next?

ten butterflies

10

eleven flowers

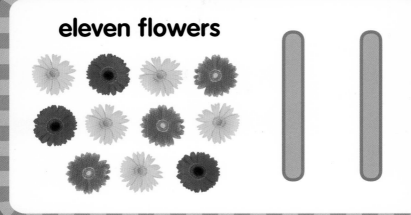

- Say the number out loud.
- Count the flowers.
- Use your finger to write the number in the air.
- How many things in this room look like a flower?
- How many pink flowers do you see?
- What number comes next?

eleven flowers

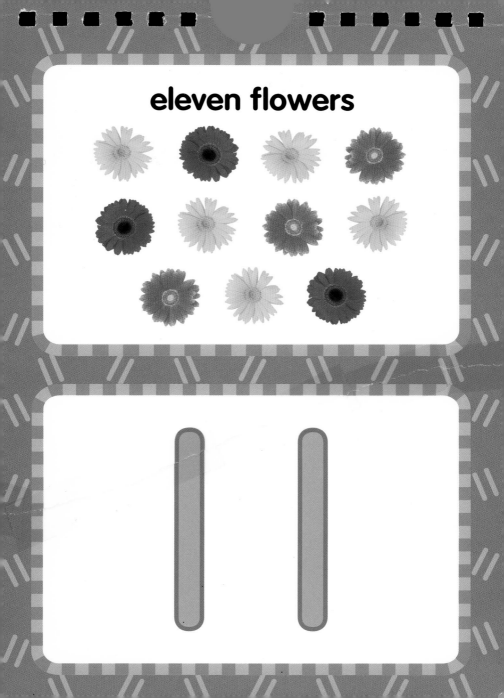

twelve feathers

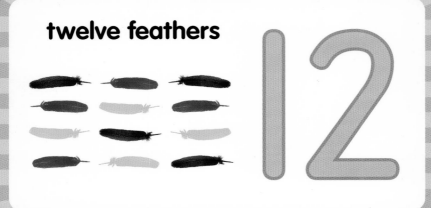

12

- Say the number out loud.
- Count the feathers.
- Use your finger to write the number in the air.
- Count backwards from 12 to 1.
- Stand on one foot and count to 12.
- What number comes next?

twelve feathers

12

thirteen badges

13

- Say the number out loud.
- Count the badges.
- Use your finger to write the number in the air.
- How many points are on each badge?
- Blink your eyes 13 times.
- What number comes next?

thirteen badges

fourteen ice-cream cones

14

- Say the number out loud.
- Count the ice-cream cones.
- Use your finger to write the number in the air.
- How many ice-cream cones would you need to feed your whole family?
- What is your favorite flavor?
- What number comes next?

fourteen ice-cream cones

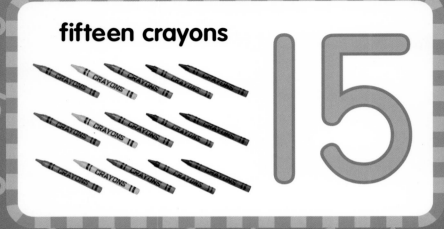

fifteen crayons

15

- Say the number out loud.
- Count the crayons.
- Use your finger to write the number in the air.
- How many different crayon colors can you count?
- What is your favorite color?
- What number comes next?

fifteen crayons

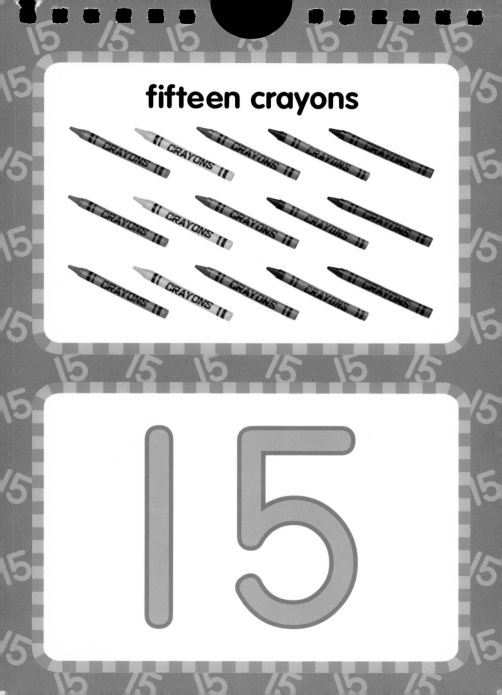

sixteen strawberries

- Say the number out loud.
- Count the strawberries.
- Use your finger to write the number in the air.
- Count the red objects in this room.
- How many other types of fruit can you think of?
- What number comes next?

sixteen strawberries

16

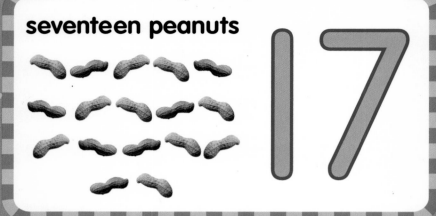

seventeen peanuts

17

- Say the number out loud.

- Count the peanuts.

- Use your finger to write the number in the air.

- Count out loud from 10 to 17.

- Do you know how many nuts are inside each peanut shell?

- What number comes next?

seventeen peanuts

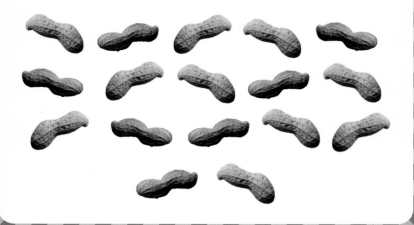

17

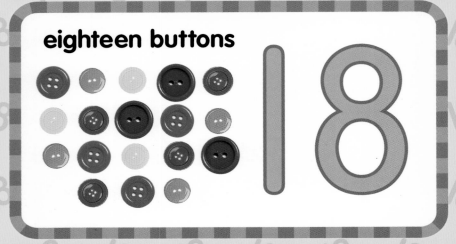

eighteen buttons

18

- Say the number out loud.
- Count the buttons.
- Use your finger to write the number in the air.
- How many blue buttons can you count?
- Are you wearing buttons? How many?
- What number comes next?

eighteen buttons

18

nineteen coins

19

- Say the number out loud.
- Count the coins.
- Use your finger to write the number in the air.
- Let's look for some real coins to count.
- How many pennies can you count here?
- What number comes next?

nineteen coins

19

twenty pieces of popcorn

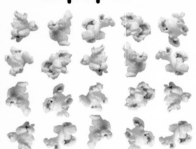

20

- Say the number out loud.
- Count the pieces of popcorn.
- Use your finger to write the number in the air.
- Count from 1 to 20.
- Let's find things on which the number 20 is written.
- What number comes next?

twenty pieces of popcorn

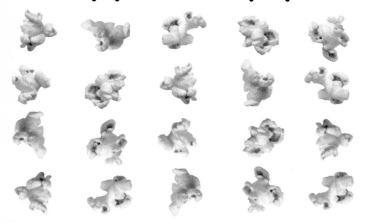

20

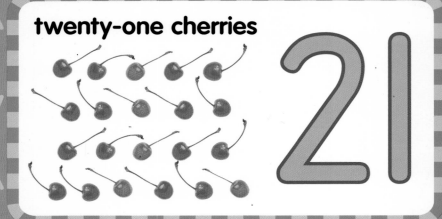

twenty-one cherries

21

- Say the number out loud.
- Count the cherries.
- Use your finger to write the number in the air.
- Try to count backwards from 21 to 1.
- Stamp your feet 21 times.
- What number comes next?

twenty-one cherries

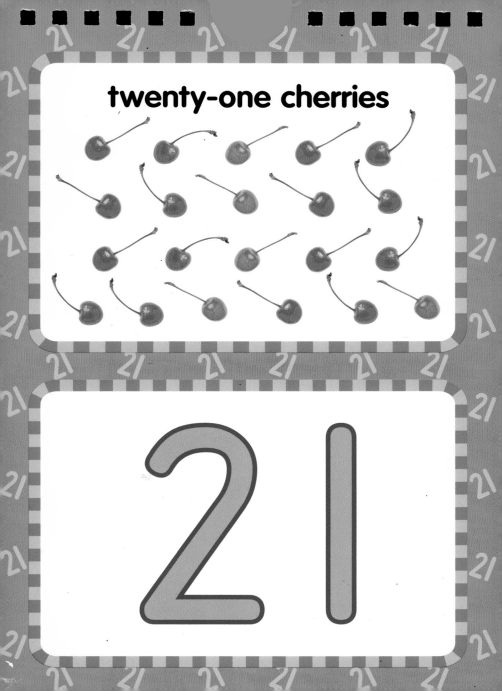

2 1

twenty-two acorns

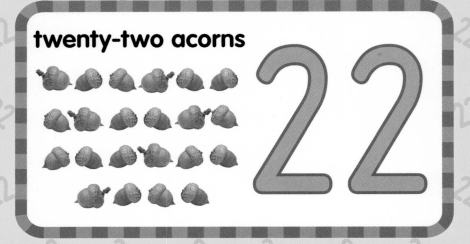

22

- Say the number out loud.
- Count the acorns.
- Use your finger to write the number in the air.
- Where do acorns come from?
- Look out your window and see how many trees you can count.
- What number comes next?

twenty-two acorns

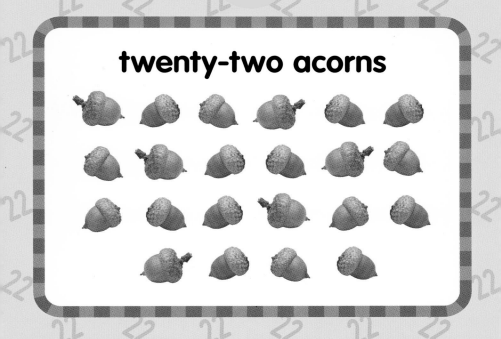

twenty-three jelly beans

23

- Say the number out loud.
- Count the jelly beans.
- Use your finger to write the number in the air.
- How many green jelly beans can you count?
- Clap your hands 23 times.
- What number comes next?

twenty-three jelly beans

23

twenty-four seeds

24

- Say the number out loud.
- Count the seeds.
- Use your finger to write the number in the air.
- How many rows of seeds can you count?
- What kind of seeds would you like to plant?
- What number comes next?

twenty-four seeds

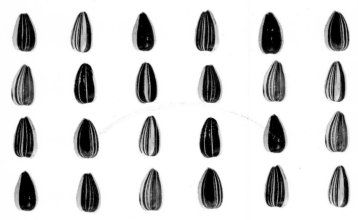

2 4

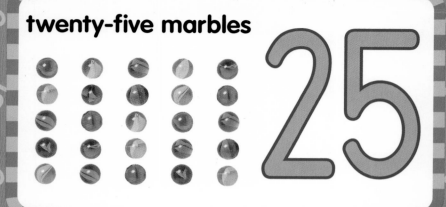

twenty-five marbles

25

- Say the number out loud.

- Count the marbles.

- Use your finger to write the number in the air.

- Count from 1 to 25.

- What do you think you'll be doing when you are 25 years old?

- What number comes next?

twenty-five marbles

1-12
review

1 2 3
4 5 6
7 8 9
10 11 12

- Count from 1 to 12.
- Count backwards from 12 to 1.
- How would a dog sound if it were to count to twelve? How about a cat? Duck? Cow?
- Let's see how many of these numbers we can find on objects around the house.
- Find some string that you can bend and twist into the shape of all these numbers.
- Think of some things that you wish you had 12 of.